W9-CAJ-712

On
top
of the
potty

To Rose and our wonderful kids,
who make every day a potty
—A. K.

To Arnie, the plumber
—D. C.

Margaret K. McElderry Books * An imprint of Simon & Schuster Children's Publishing Division * 1230 Avenue of the Americas, New York, New York 10020 * Text copyright © 2008 by Alan Katz * Illustrations copyright © 2008 by David Catrow * All rights reserved, including the right of reproduction in whole or in part in any form. * Book design by Sonia Chaghatzbanian * The text for this book is set in Kosmik. * The illustrations are rendered in watercolors, colored pencil, and ink. * Manufactured in China * 10 9 8 7 6 5 4 3 2 1 * Library of Congress Cataloging-in-Publication Data * Katz, Alan. * On top of the potty: and other get-up-and-go songs / by Alan Katz ; illustrated by David Catrow. — 1st ed. p. cm. Summary: Well-known songs with new lyrics encourage toddlers to trade in their diapers for the potty-chair, including "If You Gotta Go Do Poopy," sung to the tune of "If You're Happy and You Know It." ISBN-13: 978-0-689-86215-1 * ISBN-10: 0-689-86215-6 1. Children's songs, English—United States—Texts. 2. Toilet training—Songs and music—Texts. [1. Toilet training—Songs and music. 2. Songs.] I. Catrow, David, ill. II. Title. PZ8.3.K12750n 2008 * 782.42—dc22 [E] * 2007009004

FIRST
EDITION

On top of the potty

and other get-up-and-go songs

Alan Katz

David Catrow

Margaret K. McElderry Books
New York   London   Toronto   Sydney

If You Gotta Go Do Poopy

(To the tune of "If You're Happy and You Know It")

If you gotta go do poopy
Please don't wait
If ya gotta go do poopy
Potty's great
Uncle Sidney and Aunt Dotty
Always always use the potty
Although not at the same time
They alternate!

If you gotta go do pee-pee
Potty-chair
If ya gotta go do pee-pee
Potty's there
You will get real good with practice
And the happy happy fact is
You can trade your diapers in for
Underwear!

The Small Kids in France

(To the tune of "Home on the Range")

The small kids in France
Go *oui-oui* in their pants
And their folks toss their diapers away.

In Sydney, it's true
Kids down under go poo
And they switch to the potty one day.

All Earth kids agree
~~Pee~~ and poopers should all use potty
Yes, throughout Madrid, Spain
Kids are all potty trained
They yell *sí-sí* each time they si-ssy!

Tinkle, Tinkle on the Floor

(To the tune of "Twinkle, Twinkle, Little Star")

Tinkle, tinkle on the floor
That's what Bob did till age four
And he pooped on the den chair,
On the couch, or anywhere
He'd poop on your welcome mat,
On your swing, or on your cat.

Bob's mom said, "Please try the bowl.
Potty using is your goal."
Bob tried, and real soon he knew
Potty sitting's fun to do
As for tinkle on the floor
Bob won't do that anymore!

It's Potty Party Day

(To the tune of "Ta-Ra-Ra Boom-De-Ay")

It's potty party day
Throw my diapers away
I'm gonna use the chair
Just watch me pee in there!

It's potty party day
This stuff is child's play
I'm all grown-up, you know
So potty's where I'll go!

Oops, I can't go today
Let's party anyway
I'll learn without a doubt
(Don't throw my diapers out!)

Save potty party day
Until another day
And pretty soon I should
Be trained for good!

Training? No Complaining!

(To the tune of "This Old Man")

My friend Mike
Just went poop
On his next-door-neighbor's stoop
There's no problem
'Cause they know
He's getting potty trained
And this whole week it has rained.

My friend Hal's
Training too
And he pee-peed on his shoe
But his mom wasn't mad
Changed his shoe without a squawk
(Think she also changed his sock!)

If you go
In your pants
You'll soon get
Another chance
You can go to the potty
Whether morning, noon, or night
Next time, you will get it right.

Everyone in Nursery School

(To the tune of "Oats, Peas, Beans, and Barley Grow")

Everyone in nursery school
Sits down on the potty stool
If you join us, we know you'll
Think that potty going's cool!

First Rebecca took a turn
She was trying hard to learn
When she went, she was upset
'Cause she got her dress all wet!

Nathan did just one small drop
Then got up, he thought he'd stop
Oops, a sploosh and a kerplop
Teacher ran to get the mop!

David tried a big folks' stall
When he peed, he hit the wall
Sprayed all over our pal Paul
Man, did Paul and David bawl!

Some of us know how to go
Some of us will take it slow
When I sit, look out below
'Cause on potty I'm a pro!

Don't Flush Strange Things in the Potty

(To the tune of "The Battle Hymn of the Republic")

Don't take your sister's rattle and just drop it in the bowl
It's not a place to hide things like a pocket or a hole
It's also not a home to give your fishy or tadpole
The toilet is for poop!

Don't put your toy in the toilet
Or it's probably gonna spoil it
And your mom'll have to boil it
The toilet is for poop!

A kid I know took both his boots and flushed 'em on a whim
Then he took his favorite bear and taught him how to swim
The potty started flooding and they called on Plumber Jim
He had to fix their bowl!

Don't flush strange things in the potty
Doing that is really naughty
Pee and poop come from your body
And they go in the bowl!

People Poopy

(To the tune of "London Bridge Is Falling Down")

People poopy
Squooshy brown
Throughout town
King and clown
When they go, they flush it down
So long, poopy!

People pee-pee
With control
In the hole
On the bowl
Every single living soul
Flushes pee-pee!

Pee and poopy
Every day
That's the way
Come what may
Go and then flush it away
We'll yell, "Whoopee!"

WATCH YOUR ROYAL STEP

↑   ↑

UP

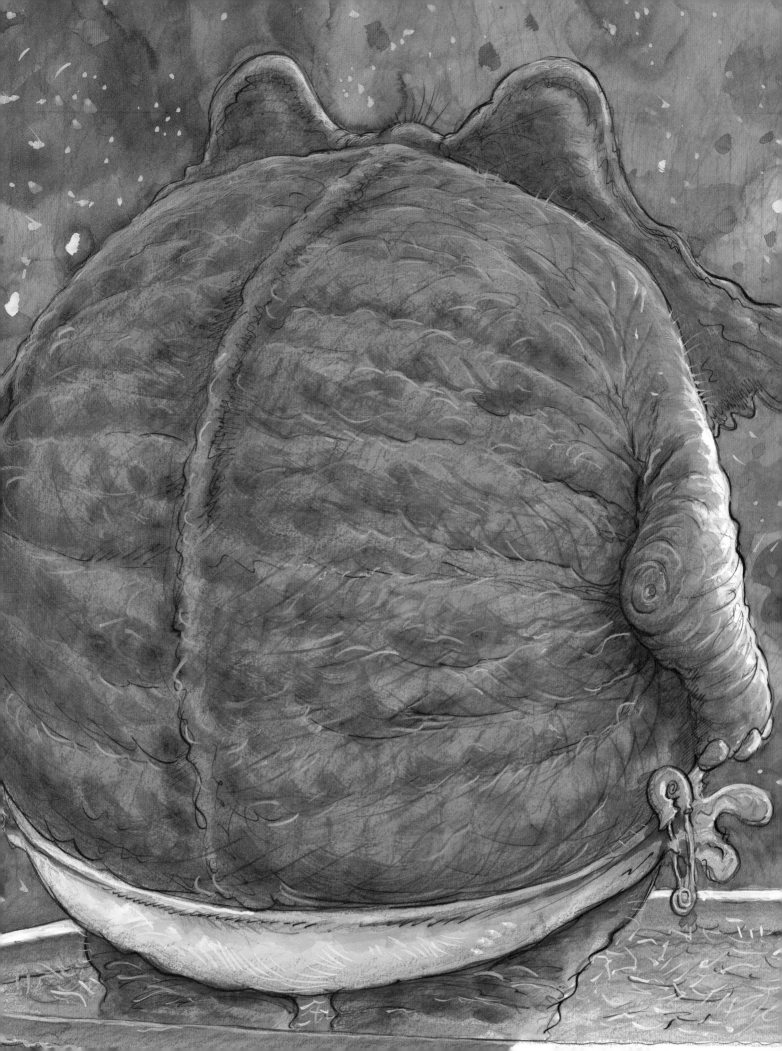

The Elephant Cried at the Circus

(To the tune of "My Bonnie Lies Over the Ocean")

The elephant cried at the circus
He said, "It is not not not fair!
The thing that just drives me berserk is
I cannot use a potty-chair!
Potty, potty
I wish I could use one to poop, to poop
Potty, potty
But they're too low and I can't stoop!"

His three-year-old friend heard him crying
Said, "I've got a potty, so what?
My diaper is fine, I'm not trying
To go on that silly old pot!
Potty, potty
I just do not need one to poop, to poop
Potty, potty
I'm not in the potty-chair group!"

"I wish I were you and not me, pal,"
The elephant sniffed and explained,
"But I'd be so happy if you shall
Agree to go get potty trained!"

Potty, potty
That's what the boy did for his friend, his friend
Potty, potty
He goes all the time
That's the end!

Scrub, Scrub, Scrub
Your Hands

(To the tune of "Row, Row, Row Your Boat")

Scrub
Scrub
Scrub your hands
Each time that you pee
That's a big-kid thing to do
When you go potty!

Don't
Don't
Don't forget
Scrub with soap, then rinse
No one likes a kid who leaves
Poopy fingerprints!

Scrub
Scrub
Scrub with soap
Each time that you poop
Nasty germs will jump off you
And they'll fly the coop!

Frankie Noodle

(To the tune of "Yankee Doodle")

Frankie Noodle
Sat right down
Right upon the potty
And he made a pee and poop
In front of everybody!

Frankie Noodle
What a kid
Everyone was clappin'
Bet you can't guess what he did
Or what else soon would happen!

Frankie Noodle
Stood and bowed
But he wasn't done there
To the horror of the crowd
He sprayed on everyone there!

Here's the lesson
I have learned
Thanks to that small fella
Watching someone potty train
Don't forget your umbrella!

I'm a Big Kid

(To the tune of "The Alphabet Song")

I'm a big kid
Almost three
And I need to go potty
But I can't
'Cause you see
On it now
Is Aunt Dee
Boy, I wish she'd move along
I can't hold it this whole song!

I've been knocking
On the door
But she says, "Two minutes more"
I can't wait
Woe is me
Let me in
Let me pee
If I must go on the floor
This house'll be a reservoir!

Here she comes
Oh hi, Aunt Dee
Guess that means
The bathroom's free
I will use
The potty
And you can take this from me
I'll stay here, yes, have no doubt
I am never coming out!

On Top of the Potty

(To the tune of "On Top of Old Smokey")

On top of the potty
It really is neat
You pee-pee or poopy
On a comfortable seat.

Sometimes it comes quickly
Sometimes it is slow
This time it's been hours
I've been waiting to go.

On top of the potty
It kind of feels weird
By the time that I finish
I might have a beard.

I think I heard something
Go dribble-y drop
And something else go like
Ker-plibitty-plop!

My daddy and mommy
Just hollered and whooped
'Cause finally, oh, finally
I pee-peed and pooped!

Go Do Poop in the Toilet

(To the tune of "Take Me Out to the Ballgame")

Go do poop in the toilet
Go do pee in the bowl
Don't have to wait till the whole thing's filled
Just go a little, we'll all be so thrilled
So please poop poop poop when you feel it
Just sit and let pee-pee flow
You're so big
And the potty is
Where all big kids go!

Go and try when you're ready
Sit whenever you're set
Do a whole pail full, or just a cup
And if you spill some, we'll clean it right up
Hey, it's not a race, so don't worry
Just take as long as you need
And you'll feel so good when you get to say,
"Look, I peed!"